W9-ATT-541

HOBBY

HOBBY

The Young Merlin Trilogy

B O O K T W O

JANE YOLEN

BENNINGTON FREE LIBRARY

Harcourt Brace & Company

SAN DIEGO   NEW YORK   LONDON

Copyright © 1996, 1986 by Jane Yolen

All rights reserved. No part of this publication may be reproduced or transmitted in any form or by any means, electronic or mechanical, including photocopy, recording, or any information storage and retrieval system, without permission in writing from the publisher.

Requests for permission to make copies of any part of the work should be mailed to: Permissions Department, Harcourt Brace & Company, 6277 Sea Harbor Drive, Orlando, Florida 32887-6777.

Acknowledgment
This book is loosely based on the short story "Dream Reader" from the collection *Merlin's Booke*, but has been significantly expanded, refocused, and changed.

Library of Congress Cataloging-in-Publication Data
Yolen, Jane.
Hobby: the young Merlin trilogy/Jane Yolen.—1st ed.
p. cm.
Sequel to: Passager.
Summary: Young Merlin is orphaned by a fire and joins a traveling pair of magicians who help him begin to discover his true powers.
ISBN 0-15-200815-2
1. Merlin (Legendary character)—Juvenile fiction. [1. Merlin (Legendary character)—Fiction. 2. Magicians—Fiction. 3. Dreams—Fiction.] I. Title.
PZ7.Y78Hn 1996
[Fic]—dc20   95–36735

Text set in Fairfield Medium
Designed by Kaelin Chappell
Printed in the United States of America
First edition
A C E F D B

For Deborah and Robert Harris
and their boys

CONTENTS

Hobby:

A small Old World falcon
or hawk that has been trained
and flown at small birds.

HOBBY

Dark.

Night.

The boy dreams of a bird, its breast as red as flames, rising to heaven singing, and wakes to smoke.

Fire licks the edges of the thatched rooftop, bright shooting stars let loose from a chink in the chimney. The house is suddenly aglow.

A dog howls.

Then a second.

Bells from the mews jangle frantically.

The scream of a woman tears the air. "Master Robin. Master—" Her voice is cut off.

A door bursts open and a figure appears. It is a boy carrying the body of a dog. They are haloed by fire. Gently, he places the dog on the ground, well away from the flames, then turns to go back in.

Someone else stumbles through the door. A woman, by the clothes. But she has no hair, it having been consumed by the fire. The boy catches her before she falls. He lays her down by the dog's side, turns.

The roof falls in with a great whooosh *of sound. No one else alive can come out of that house. No one alive can go in.*

Sparks fly to the mews, to the barn and, like the house, they are devoured whole.

After a long while—a day, a lifetime—the flames are silent.

Birds sing from the nearby woods.

Light.

Day.

1. LIES

THE BOY BURIED THEM ALL IN A SINGLE GRAVE: dog, woman, and the charred remains of the others. Of the birds in the mews there was nothing left to bury. Nothing except one tiny brass bell from the littlest hawk's jesses. He pocketed this treasure without thinking.

A single grave. Digging five separate ones would have been too hard for him. At twelve he did not yet have his full strength. But he did it also because he could not bear that they should be apart: Master Robin, Mag, Nell, the two dogs. They were his family, all that he had had for the past four years. A family, he knew, must stay as one. He did not know how he knew it, but he did.

He would have thrown himself into the pit as well, as penance for not understanding his dream of the bird in flames and rising sooner. The guilt of all their deaths, of the fact that he was still alive, was almost too great to bear. But there was something in him, a kind of sense as strong as that of sight and hearing and smell, that told him to stay alive.

"And remember," he whispered to himself. By that he meant *remember* Master Robin, who had rescued him from the woods and taught him to read, both the words on a slate and the passage of a hawk across the sky. And remember Mag, who had kept him cosseted and fed. And Nell, who had taught him all the games he had missed as a child. And the dogs who guarded him at night and brought back thrown sticks and licked his face. And the falcons who came to his hand. If he remembered them, they would still be alive, in some odd way. Not alive *beside* him, but *inside* him.

He said a prayer over the grave, a prayer that took in the fact that though his own world seemed to have ended, the world seemed still to go on. And he spoke words he vaguely recalled in Latin, though he didn't know it was Latin he was recalling. *"In nomine Patris,"* he said.

And he told himself the first of many lies he would tell that fall. "I will not cry."

It was a lie before he left the farmsteadings.

He drove the old dry cow before him, led the great-footed mare. They had been out in the pasture and thus been spared of the fire. He wore his nightshirt tucked into a pair of singed trousers and carried the one pair of boots the fire had not taken, their lacings tied together and slung across his back. They were not his boots; his boots were ash. These were an old pair of Master Robin's boots that had been set out by the door, too dirty for Mag's fresh flooring. He would grow into them in time.

He had slaughtered the two hens, after gathering their last two eggs, because he couldn't herd them properly and didn't want to leave them for the foxes. And he cooked them on the embers of the house and mews to have food for the long walk ahead. One chicken and the eggs he finished before leaving, for grave digging was hard work and he was famished. The other chicken he put in the leather pouch, along with the little bell.

He did not know where he was going, exactly, but he could not bear to stay at the ruin of the farm. Once he had gone to a great fair with Master Robin and it had been several days' walk west. If he could find it again, he thought he might sell both cow and horse there and make a new life on his own.

Chewing thoughtfully on a drumstick, the boy turned to look one last time at the burned-out hulk that had been his home for four years. *That* was when he began to cry, the tears falling quickly.

But he did not make a sound as he cried. He was afraid if he started, his howling would never stop.

The woods were cold and spattered with sunlight wherever the interlacings of yellowing leaves thinned out. For a while he rode the horse, a big-hearted Dales mare named Goodie. She had a walk better suited to the plow and he had to ride her bareback. Still, he was such a light weight, she hardly noticed him.

The cow plodded placidly behind the horse. They made an uncommon pair, but so long together in the same barn and pasture, they were as easy with one another as old gossips. The boy napped twice on the horse's back. Each small sleep brought him the same snippet of dream: the flame-breasted bird singing of danger. He forced himself to wake and mourned his lost family at each waking.

By nightfall, not only the leaves had thinned out, but the trees as well. The boy got off the horse, leading both horse and cow behind by their halter ropes. He did not want to chance that either might run off, startled by some new sight or sound.

The broad and knotted holm oaks gave way to a large meadow. Still in the oak shadow, the boy listened intently to a stirring of nearby grasses.

Suddenly a herd of deer, small and brown and dappled with moonlight, passed by so close to him, he could see their liquid eyes. Goodie whinnied and, at that, the deer were gone, as if by magic.

Magic! For a moment the boy wondered if the deer were a sign. But though he was used to dreams, both waking and sleeping, he had never dreamed of deer. He let out a deep breath, which surprised him, for he had not known he was hold-ing it.

"Now, Goodie," he said to the horse. "Now, Churn," to the cow. "We must rest the night. I promise you will be safe."

He tied them loosely to a low tree branch, then settled himself up in the crotch of one of the oaks.

"I am too tired to dream," he called down to them, hoping that by saying the words aloud they would become true. He was afraid to dream again of the fire bird, afraid to be reminded once more how his refusal to wake in time, his inability to understand the dream in time, had robbed him of his family. "I will not let myself dream," he called to the horse and cow.

Another lie.

2. WALLS

HE DREAMED OF HOME. NOT THE HOME HE HAD last seen, burned and blackened, but a different home. This one was stone upon stone, several towers high, with tile roofs and stone walkways. Only women lived there, dressed like crows. They pecked at him with tiny, quick beaks. They beat at him with black wings. Then, at a high-pitched whistle, they left off abusing him and rose into the air, circling the towers and then down to a courtyard where a priest dressed in black called them down like a falconer.

The boy woke, shivering, and for a moment was eight years old again, alone and in the forest. "Horse," he reminded himself, staring down into the darkness. "Cow." They had been among his first words when Master Robin rescued him. Then he mumbled his own name and, with that, fell asleep once again to dream—as boys often do—of dragons.

When he woke for good, it was dawn. Birdsong assaulted him. From the tree he could look far across the meadow to a sudden blue lake, winking in the light, like a signal lantern. To the right of the lake was a swath of sandy shingle. To the left was something very like a high wall.

"A wall," he said aloud. "A wall means people." It had to be a town's gate. The town he and Master Robin had visited. He smiled and, still sitting in the tree, fetched out the last pieces of chicken from his leather pouch. There was no need to keep them any longer, for there would be food aplenty in the town. He ate contentedly.

When he was done, he rubbed his sleeve across his greasy mouth. He thought that Mag would have clapped him hard on the ear for so doing. She had cloths at the table for such. How often had she told him: "Easier to wash them, than to wash thy shirt, boy."

But he had no table cloths. And no wash water.

And no Mag either. The thought threatened to unman him once again and, in order not to cry, he leaped down from the tree. He hit the ground solidly, frightening the cow but not the stolid Goodie, who only shook her head in annoyance.

If he wished for a cloth, he wished even more for some drinking water, for the chicken had awakened a sudden thirst in him. But his skin bag was empty. Still, ahead lay the lake and the wall, the one meaning water and the other company. He got up on Goodie's back and, holding Churn's long halter rope, pulled her after them, though she clearly wanted to browse the meadow.

No amount of kicking with his bare heels moved Goodie out of her walk, and so the boy relaxed and watched as swallows crisscrossed before them, chasing after insects the horse and cow kicked up.

It took them the greater part of an hour to get close enough to see that the wall was not part of a town but marked the site of a large ruin. They picked their way carefully through the debris of some old outworks, the broken weedy remains of a road. Goodie stepped high over the crumbled stones. The boy had to yank several times hard on the cow's rope to encourage her to follow. But when at last there was a wind off the lake and she smelled the water, Churn picked up her legs in a fast trot, suddenly almost young again.

At the lake's edge, the two animals drank eagerly. But after a handful of water, the boy went over to the ruins, curiosity getting the better of thirst.

There was a series of high walls, all broken at the top, though several half-roofs of dark tile still guarded the upper rooms from weather. At his approach, a dozen doves clattered up into the light, proving that the place was long deserted.

The ruins reminded him, oddly enough, of his dream: the same high walls, the half-gabled roofs. They lacked only the crow women in their black robes, and the priest. He wondered what people had lived in this place and for a moment closed his eyes, as if that could help him envision them. But he could not imagine anyone here. It was too long empty. Too musty. Too cold.

He stepped over some broken stones and found himself in a kind of courtyard, clearly once a garden, for there were several ancient fruit trees bent like old men, the browned remains of unharvested fruit by the twisted roots. Stones lined out a series of still-neat borders but nettles had taken over the plots of earth. In the very center of the garden was a mosaic, partially covered with dirt and uneven where the ground had shifted beneath it. The boy could make out some sort of spade-bearded, fish-tailed god; it looked a lot like Master Robin, broad shouldered and with red-brown hair. The boy turned away quickly before he had time to weep, his hand going to the leather pocket where the hawk's bell rested.

It was when he stepped through two massive upright pillars, grooved by human hand and pitted by wind and storms, that he smelled something that was neither meadow, nor lake, nor the musty, stale scent of the ruins.

It was smoke.

3. SMOKE

HE KNEW THAT SMELL. NOT THE ODOR OF A house burning down, still so fresh and bitter to him. It was the smell of a cookfire, with meat on a spit.

This time, though, caution claimed him. He crept to the side of the garden wall and, using it to shield his back, inched up a set of stone steps that were still preserved and whole.

At the top the stairs broke off awkwardly, but the boy could look down over the entire ruins. He saw the cookfire. It was in one of a series of out-lying half-roofed houses beyond the main walls. A man dressed all in black was poking at the fire with a stick. He reminded the boy of the priest in his dream.

The boy almost called out then, but there was something about the man's shoulders he did not care for, a tense roundness, like a hawk right before it mantled, throwing one wing out, then another, to protect its food. Those shoulders belonged to a greedy, angry man, the boy thought. He needed to find people, but—even more—he needed to be careful.

Taking his bearings, the boy ran back down the stairs, turned in through a massive archway, and threaded his way as quietly as possible through the remains of the halls, now only broken masonry and vines.

When he found the cookfire, more by smell than by the mapping in his head, creeping up to peer through the doorway, the man was gone. A rabbit roasting on a spit was not quite done.

He heard a low growl behind him and slowly turned.

In the ruined hallway, glaring at him, was a massive dark dog, its teeth bared.

The boy backed up a step, toward the spit, and moving very slowly, took the boots from around his neck. They were the closest thing to a weapon he had. He was about to fling them at the dog when a whistle shrilled through the air and the dog's ears raised.

"Hold, Ranger!" came a coarse, raw-edged voice from beyond the doorway, and the dog's legs tensed, though it did not otherwise move.

The man stepped into view with hair the grey of old bowstring and a sparse, tired mustache. One eye was half shuttered by scarring. He wiped his nose with his black sleeve but never took his eye off the boy. "Watch!" he commanded the dog.

"Sir . . ." the boy began, knowing full well the man was no kind of gentry by his voice and clothes. Still, he did not want to provoke the man; he had no idea how dangerous the man was. "Sir, help me. I have been burned out of my house. My family died in the fire. And I am . . ."

"I think you are a thief, boy. Those boots you hold are much too big for you. That horse and cow too rich for such as you. I think you should be taken to the local sheriff and . . ."

"I think you are, yourself, a thief and shall not take me there," the boy answered hotly.

The man laughed briefly and horribly, then took two large steps forward so that the boy could smell his terrible breath. He grabbed the boy's shoulder. "Thief I may sometimes be," he said, his raw voice still full of the laugh, "but I will not be called so by a mere boy." In one swift move, he ripped the boots from the boy's hands and threw him down, kicking him in the side almost as an afterthought. It was not hard enough to break any bones, only hard enough to show who was master.

"Ranger," the man said, "keep!"

The dog stood over the boy, growling in a quiet monotone.

"Ranger will not hurt you, boy," the man said with a chuckle. "Lest, of course, you move." He bent over and tore the leather pocket from the boy's side. Opening it, he found only the charred bell, greasy from chicken, and threw it on the ground in disgust.

The boy bit his lip to keep from crying out; the loss of the little hawk's bell hurt more than the kick had.

Sitting down at the fire, the man took off his own boots, which were scarcely more than two pieces of leather tied onto the foot. Slipping on Master Robin's boots, he sighed. "Just my size," he said, and laughed again. "Or close enough that makes no difference. One's not a man without proper boots, don't you think?" He stretched his long legs closer to the fire and sniffed the air appreciatively. "Rabbit's about done, boy. If you lie quiet, I might just give you a piece."

"I want none of you," the boy said. "Or your rabbit." His bravado was encouraged by the fact that his own belly was full enough with chicken. But when he spoke, the dog growled again and moved, if possible, even closer to him, its breath as bad as its master's.

"Not now, perhaps," the man said. "But anon." He began to eat greedily, smacking his lips as he did so. His manners, the boy thought, would have earned him a great clap on the head from Mag.

The boy lay still, ribs aching, and fell into a kind of reverie. In it he saw the man felled by a thrown stone, crumpling to the ground, where he lay haloed in blood. A dog licked the blood till it was gone, then put its reddened muzzle into the air and howled. But when the boy woke, the man was very much alive and the dog had not moved from its guard position. Then the boy knew that it had just been a dream. His eyes began to tear up and he willed himself not to cry.

4. FOR SALE

THEY STAYED IN THE RUINS FOR THE REST OF that day and night. Much of the time the boy was bound, loosely when the dog was nearby, tightly when it was gone hunting with the man. No amount of twisting and rubbing the rope against stone seemed to help.

The boy fell to dreaming more and more, and his dreams were of blood and fire, fire and blood. They exhausted him. They confused him. He wondered if they had any meaning beyond disturbing his sleep.

At dawn the man seemed to make up his mind about something. "Not coming then," he mused aloud. "Well, it was worth the try."

"What was?" the boy asked, thinking the man was speaking to him, and receiving a cuff on the ear for asking. It was hard enough to make him fall over, hard enough to set his ear ringing, like the bells of a captive hawk.

The man picked him up, setting him against a fallen pillar. "Now, boy, don't ask me questions. I do not like it. Give me answers. That will sweeten my hand."

The boy nodded, not chancing another blow.

"What is your name then, little thief?"

The boy thought for a moment. His name was Merlin, like the hawk in Master Robin's mews. But that was his name with the family. And the family was no more, buried under earth and gone to worms. Names could have power, he knew that instinctively. His own name had given him back his power of speech, had given him a past. And even though this man's power was great, it was a black, evil thing. He would give the man no more power than he already had.

"Hawk," the boy said. "My name is Hawk." It was close enough.

The man laughed. "A lie of course. You hesitated too long for the truth. And who would have named such a small, darkling boy such a strong, powerful name? But no matter. I will call you Hawk. It is conveniently short. And as for me, you can call me . . . Fowler . . . for I have mastered you as a falconer does a bird."

The boy almost spoke back then, for if he knew anything well from his years with Master Robin it was falconry. This man was no fowler. And he was no master either. But the boy bit his lip and said nothing.

"We are but a day out of Gwethern, a busy little market town, where I will sell your labor to a farmer and collect the wages. And you will not run, little bird, else I will have the sheriff on you. As will the farmer." He smiled. It did not improve his looks. "Do you understand me?"

The boy glared.

Fowler raised his hand for a slap.

"Yes," Hawk said, begrudging the syllable.

"Yes what?"

"Yes . . . sir." The second syllable was even more grudging.

"I will unbind you, hawkling," Fowler said. "But my dog will be your leading strings. Mind him, now. He has a foul temper. Fowler and Fouler."

He laughed at his own joke, the sound coming out jerkily.

Hawk did not smile. He stood slowly and held out his hands. Fowler undid the ropes on the boy's wrists.

"Watch!" he said to the dog, and Ranger took up a position at Hawk's heels. He did not leave that place for the rest of the long day.

They walked for a while before Fowler mounted Goodie. The big horse trembled under his weight, not because the man was heavy but because he was unfamiliar and kept at her with his rough boot heels.

They made a strange company, but not so unusual for a market town road: a half-grown boy, nervously in front of a menace of a dog; a massive, black-clad man on a plowhorse, leading an old cow by a rope.

No one will wonder about us, Hawk realized. *No one will question the man's right to sell us all: horse, cow, boy. Even dog.*

Just as he came to that awful conclusion, a large tan hare started across the road.

"Ranger, stay!" Fowler called out, though the dog had made no move toward the hare. But Fowler should have paid more mind to the horse. Unused to the road, upset with the man on her back, startled by the hare, the normally placid Goodie suddenly shied. She took one quick step to the left and then rose up onto her back legs.

Fowler was flung off, landing with a horrifying *thud!* His head whacked against a marker stone and, as he lay there, unmoving, blood flowed out of his nose, staining his mustache.

The dog left the boy's heels and went over to its master. It sniffed the man's head uncertainly, then sat down, threw back its head, and howled.

For a moment Hawk did not know what to do. He was stunned by the scene, which was— and was not—the very dream he had had: stone, blood, howl. He remembered, bleakly, the other dreams he had had that had come true. The dream of the flame-breasted bird. The dream of the whistling black-coated man. And now, most horribly specific, this.

He did not know if his dreams were wishes so powerful they came true, though he had certainly never wanted the fire that had destroyed his life. He did not know if he had the ability to see slant-wise into the future. Either—or both. He did not know and was afraid to know.

The dog kept on howling, an eerie sound, awful and final.

And tears, unwanted, uncalled-for, fell from Hawk's eyes. He could not seem to stop crying.

5. THE TOWN

"WHY?" HAWK ASKED ALOUD. BY THAT HE MEANT: Why was he crying at the death of the awful Fowler, a man who had beaten him and tied him up and would have sold him? Why was he crying now when he had not cried—not really—at the death of those he loved? Master Robin, Mag, Nell, the dogs, the hawks. "Why?"

Still crying, he got up onto Goodie's back, for she was once again the stolid plowhorse, and they started down the road, with Churn right after.

Hawk wiped his nose on the back of his sleeve, thinking that he had not been able to touch the man nor bring himself to bury him. He only wanted to be gone away, from the man, the stone, the blood, the howls. He was almost a mile along before he could no longer hear the dog.

Without wanting to, Hawk fell into a reverie on Goodie's back and began to daydream. It was a very odd dream this time—of a wizard and a green castle. There was a bird in the dream as well, eating an apple, then spitting out a green worm. When the worm touched the ground, it grew to dragon size, then took to the air, its great wings whipping up a wind. Hawk woke sweating, though the day was cool. Was it another dream of the future? And what future, he wondered, could include all those things?

As suddenly as the dream ended, so did the path. It opened instead onto a real road that was rutted with use. For the first time there were other travelers: farmers with carts piled high with vegetables—carrots and neeps and green onions. Whole families in wagons, the children packed in with the caged fowl. Here and there single riders trotted on fine horses, not plowmares like Goodie. Hawk felt entirely awkward and dirty, ragged and alone. But at least he saw nothing like a wizard, a castle, an apple, or a worm.

26

He was hungry, but there was little he could do about it until they came upon a town. Besides, hunger was not new to him. Before he had found his family, he lived alone in the woods for a year, foraging for berries and nuts. He had not starved. One or two days without a proper meal would not kill him. Fire killed. Men killed. His own belly would not do him in.

He guessed he should have turned out Fowler's pockets. A dead man spends no coins. But that would have made him a thief indeed, and despite what Fowler had called him, he was none of that.

The road quite suddenly widened and ahead was the town. He recognized its gate. It seemed even grander than he remembered, made grander perhaps by his hunger and his fears. He let Goodie go her own pace, following after the wagons and carts, in through the stone gate marked with the town's seal. Gwethern.

Clearly it was a market day. Stalls lined the high street. There was more food—and more people—than Hawk had seen in a year. His stomach proclaimed his hunger loudly. But it proclaimed something else as well, a kind of ache that food would not take away. To buy food, he had to sell either Churn or Goodie, and they were his last ties to the farm. He got off the horse's back and led both horse and cow carefully through the crowded street.

Noise surrounded him: sellers calling out their wares, children whining for a sweet, women arguing over the price of a bit of cloth, a tinker bargaining with a man for a wild-eyed mare, a troubadour tuning his lute, two farmers arguing over stall space, and a general low hubbub.

For a boy used to living on a small quiet farm near a wood, it was suddenly too much, and Hawk backed up as if to escape it all, bumping into a barrow full of yellow apples.

"You! Boy!" came a shout from behind the barrow.

Hawk turned. There was a man with a face as yellow and sunken as any old apple; veins large as worm runnels crossed his nose.

Startled, Hawk stepped back against Goodie's shoulder and the man slammed a stick down across the barrow. If it had landed on Hawk, it would have been a sharp and painful blow.

"If you do not mean to buy, boy, you cannot touch."

"I . . . I . . ." Hawk began, suddenly remembering his strange dream about the apple.

"How do you know he does not mean to buy?" asked a voice behind him. Hawk was afraid to turn around in case the apple man struck out again, this time landing a blow.

"This rag of cloth hung on bones?" The apple cart man laughed. "He's no mother's son, by the dirt on him. A devil's spawn rather. Where would he get any coins?"

"You think he's a beggar? With that horse and cow?"

This time Hawk dared to look at his rescuer. The man was dressed in an outlandish blue cloak and feathered hat, like a mountebank.

"And as for that horse and cow . . ." the apple-faced man was saying, "where do you suppose he got them, the cheeky beggar."

"Right," the cloaked man said. "Cheeky indeed. And that's where he keeps his coin. In his cheek!" He laughed a sharp, yipping sound, which drew an appreciative chuckle from the crowd just starting to gather around them. Entertainment in any town being a rare commodity, even on market fair day, the folk of Gwethern were more than willing to egg on a fight.

"Open your mouth, boy, and give the man his coin."

Hawk was so surprised, his mouth dropped open on its own and a coin seemed to fall from his lips into the cloaked man's hand.

"Here," the man said, flipping the coin into the air. It turned twice over before the apple cart man grabbed it up, bit it, grunted, and shoved it into his purse.

The cloaked man picked out two yellow apples and placed one in each of Hawk's hands. As he did so, he whispered, "If you wish to repay me, boy, look for the green wagon, the castle on wheels."

Then he vanished into the crowd.

6. THE CASTLE
ON WHEELS

HAWK ATE THE TWO APPLES SLOWLY, SAVORING them. When he found a little green worm in the second one, he set the worm down carefully on a stone. It inched away, looking nothing at all like a dragon.

"Apples, worms . . . what does all this dreaming mean?" he asked himself aloud. Then he set out to look for the wagon.

It was not hard to find.

Parked under a chestnut tree, the wagon was as green as a fairy's gown. And it was indeed a castle on wheels, for the top of the wagon was vaulted over and an entire outline of a tower and keep was painted on the side. Hawk shivered. The dream, it seemed, was coming true.

Two docile, drab-colored mules were hitched to the wagon. They seemed oblivious to the sounds of the busy market day around them, contentedly nibbling on the few blades of brown grass that had managed to grow beneath the widespread tree.

Above the castle tower, on either side, were two painted figures. One was a tall, amber-eyed mage with a conical hat. The other was a dark-haired princess playing a harp.

Hawk walked quickly toward the wagon, pulling Goodie and Churn with him.

"So, boy, have you come to pay us back?" asked a soft voice. It was followed immediately by the trill of a mistle thrush.

At first he could not see who was speaking. Then something moved at one of the painted castle windows, a pale moon of a face. In a moment it had disappeared, and right after, a woman stepped through the castle door.

Hawk stared at her. She was possibly the most beautiful woman he had ever seen. She was not at all like Mag, who had been motherly and stout.

Or Nell, who had been all angles and elbows. Nor like any of the women dressed like crows in his dreams. There was not a woman he had seen at the market fair to compare with her. Her long dark hair, unbound, fell to her waist. She wore a dress of scarlet wool, and jewels in her ears that made a pleasant jangling, like a hawk's jesses. A yellow purse hung from a braided belt and it, too, jangled whenever she moved. As he watched, she bound up her hair with a single, swift motion into a net of scarlet linen.

She smiled. "Ding-dang-dong, cat's got your tongue, then?"

When he didn't answer, she laughed. But it wasn't a nasty laugh, at his expense. It was a laugh at the entire world, a laugh that invited him in. Before he could laugh back, though, she had reached back behind her and pulled out a harp, exactly like the one painted on the wagon's side. Strumming the harp with her long nails, she began to sing:

> "A boy with shirt a somber blue
> Will never ever come to rue,
> A boy with . . ."

"Are you singing about me?" asked Hawk, hoping she was.

"Do you think I am singing about you?" the woman asked, then pursed her lips and made the mistle thrush trill.

"If not now, you will someday," Hawk said. He did not know why he said it, but it seemed suddenly right, almost as if he had dreamed it.

"I believe you," said the woman, but she was busy tuning her harp at the same time. It was as if Hawk did not really exist for her except as an audience to be cozened. He was not sure he liked that.

Suddenly she stood. "You did not answer my question, boy."

"What question?"

"Have you come to pay what you owe?"

Puzzled, Hawk replied, "I did not answer because I did not know you were talking to me. I owe you nothing."

"Ah—but you owe it me," came a lower voice from inside the wagon, where it was dark. "And Viviane and I share all."

A man emerged from the wagon and, even

though he was not wearing the cloak, Hawk knew him. He was the mountebank, but he was also the mage on the wagon's side: the slate grey hair was the same. And the amber eyes.

"I do not owe you either, sir," Hawk said.

"What of the apples, boy? And the coin that fell from your mouth?"

Hawk looked straightaway into the man's eyes. "The coin was a trick. And the apples were meant to come to me, sir. I dreamed them."

The woman laughed. "Clever boy. And why did you come here to the green castle, if not to pay?" All the while she spoke, she smoothed her dress with her long slim fingers.

"As the apples were meant to come into my hands, so I believe I am to come into yours," Hawk said.

The woman laughed again, throwing her head back. The earrings and the purse jingled and jangled, as if they were laughing, too. "Only you hope," she said, suddenly quite serious, "that the mage will not eat you up and put your little green worm on a rock for some passing scavenger."

Hawk's mouth dropped open. "How did you know about the worm? About the dream?"

"Bards know everything," she said. "Everything about magic."

"And *tell* everything as well," said the mage. He clapped her lightly on the shoulder and she went, laughing and jangling, back through the wagon door.

7. THE MAGE

HAWK NODDED TO HIMSELF. "IT WAS THE WIN-
dow," he whispered at last, though the answer did
not entirely satisfy him.

"Of course it was the window," said the mage.
"And if you wish to speak to yourself so no one
else is the wiser, make it *sotto voce,* under the
breath thus." And while his lips moved, no sound
came out. "Still, a whisper is no guarantee of secrets," he laughed, "if there is one like my Viviane
who can read lips."

"Sotto voce," Hawk said aloud. And then repeated, this time soundlessly.

"The soldiers first brought the phrase from far
Rome," the mage said. "But it rides the market

roads, now. Much that is knowledge came from there. Little grows in our land but oak and thorn."

"*Sotto voce,*" Hawk repeated, punctuating his memory.

"I like you, boy," said the mage. "But then, I collect oddities."

"Did you collect the bard, sir?"

Looking quickly over his shoulder at the door into the wagon, the mage said, "Her?"

"Yes, sir."

"I did."

"How is—*she*—an oddity?" asked Hawk. "I think she is"—he took a gulp—"wonderful."

The mage smiled, as if he shared a joke with himself. "That she is. Quite wonderful, my Viviane. And well she knows it. She has a range of four octaves and can mimic any bird or beast I name." He paused. "And a few I cannot."

Hawk nodded solemnly. So solemnly, in fact, the mage laughed out loud. "You are an oddity, too, boy. I thought so when first I saw you riding through Gwethern gates, all raggedy and under-fed, yet like a prince on that plowhorse. Like a hero from one of the tales. 'There's one to watch!' I told myself."

"Sotto voce?" Hawk asked.

"Indeed. It is never good to let others in on one's secrets. So I followed you, asking about you in case there was someone who knew. But you were a mystery to everyone I asked. And then, when the apple man had at you, I saw my opportunity. You protested at neither the stick nor the coin dropping from your lips. I could feel your anger, your surprise. That calm, poised center—quite something in a boy your age. You *are* an oddity. I sniffed it out with my nose from the first. And my nose . . ." He tapped it with his forefinger, which made him look both wise and ominous at once. "My nose never lies. Do you think yourself odd?"

Hawk closed his eyes for a moment, thinking. When he opened them again, he said, "I have dreams."

The mage held his breath, a kind of innate wisdom on his part, and waited.

"I dreamed of a mage today. There was an apple and a worm in the dream as well. And a castle green as early spring grass. Now that I have seen your wagon, I know which castle. And I know you are the mage. And the green worm I myself placed upon the stone." He did not mention that it had become a dragon, thinking suddenly that it might be best to keep some of his dreaming *sotto voce*.

"Do you . . . dream . . . often?" the mage asked carefully, slowly coming down the steps of the wagon and sitting on the bottom step.

Hawk nodded.

"Tell me."

"You will think me a liar. Perhaps you will hit me," Hawk said.

This time the mage laughed out loud, with his head back, a low theatrical laugh, though Hawk —who knew nothing of the theater—did not know it as such. The mage stopped laughing and looked closely at the boy, narrowing his eyes. "I have never hit anyone in my life, boy. And telling lies is an essential part of magic. You lie with your hands, like this." So saying, he reached behind Hawk's ear and pulled out a bouquet of meadowsweet, wintergreen, and a single blue aster. "You see—my hands told the lie that flowers grow in the dirt behind your ear. And your eyes believed it. And I know you have no mother, for there is no mother who would allow such dirt to remain for long on a boy's neck."

Hawk laughed at that until he almost cried.

The mage looked away to give him time to recover, then looked back. Then he leaned forward and whispered. "But never let Viviane know we tell lies. She is as practiced in her anger as she is on her harp. *I* may never swat a liar, but she is the very devil when her temper is aroused."

"I will not," Hawk said solemnly.

"Then tell me about your dreams."

He told them, then, one after another—the fire bird, the whistling priest, the bloodied man dead by the howling dog. The mage listened quietly, leaning forward every once in a while during the telling, as if by moving closer to the boy, he moved closer to an understanding of the dreams. And when Hawk was finished speaking, the mage reached over and clasped his hand tightly. Hawk felt something in his palm and looked down. It was a small copper coin.

"Buy yourself a meat pie, boy," the mage said. "And then come along with us. There is plenty of room in the green castle and I think you, your horse, and cow will make a fine addition to our traveling show."

"Thank you, sir," Hawk said.

"Not *sir*, for pity's sake. My name is Ambrosius, because of my amber eyes. Did you notice them? Ambrosius the Wandering Mage. It says so on the other side of the wagon, but I doubt you can read."

"I can, sir. Ambrosius." Hawk smiled shyly at this revelation.

"Ah," the man said, and squinted one eye as if reassessing the boy. "And what is your name? I cannot keep calling you boy."

Hawk hesitated, looking down.

"Come, come, I will not hit you. And you may keep the coin whatever you say. Names do not matter all that much now, do they?"

But the boy knew names *did* matter. Especially around power such as the mage's. He drew in a deep breath. "My name is Hawk," he said.

"Hawk is it?" Ambrosius smiled very carefully. "Well, perhaps someday you will grow into that name. And perhaps it is your real name. But caution dictates a change of nomenclature. For the road. You are a bit thin and undersized for a hawk. Even a young hawk."

A strange, sharp cackling sound came from the interior of the wagon, a high *ki-ki-ki-ki*.

Ambrosius looked back for a moment. "Viviane says you *are* a hawk, but a small one. A hobby, perhaps."

"Hobby," the boy whispered, knowing a hobby was still larger than a merlin. His hand clutched the coin so tightly it left a mark on his palm. "Hobby."

"Good. Then it is settled," Ambrosius said, standing. "Fly off to your meat pie, Hobby, then fly quickly back to me. We travel from here on to Carmarthen fair, a rather larger town for our playing. Viviane will sing like a lark. I will do my magic. And you—well, we will figure out something quite worthy, I can promise you. There are fortunes to be made on the road, young Hobby, if you can sing in four voices and pluck flowers out of the air."

8. THE CITY

THE ROAD WAS GENTLE AND WINDING, THROUGH still-green valleys and alongside clear, quick streams full of trout. The trees were green with touches of gold, but on the far ridges the forests were already bare. Days were growing shorter and overhead the greylags, in great vees, flew south amid a tremendous noise.

As the wagon bounced along, Viviane sang songs about Robin o' the Wood in a high, sweet voice, and about the Battle of the Trees in a voice that was low and thrilling. In a middle voice, rather like Hobby's own, she sang a lusty song about a bold warrior and a peasant maid that turned his cheeks pink and hot.

Ambrosius shortened the journey with his spirited tellings of wonder tales and histories, though which was which was sometimes hard to tell. There was the story of a wolf who suckled a pair of human twins, a great leader named Julius murdered by his friends, and another leader who had played on his lute while his city burned. This last was rather too close to Hobby's own history and he had to look away for a moment. When he looked back, it was to watch Ambrosius make coins walk across his knuckles. Then, almost as an afterthought, the mage reached into Hobby's shirt and drew out a turtledove. It surprised the bird even more than the boy, and the dove flew off onto a low branch of an ash tree and plucked at its feathers furiously until the wagon, trailing the horse and cow, had passed by.

They were two days traveling, wonderful days for Hobby. He felt content, caring little if they ever arrived at the city. At night he did not dream.

In between the two travel days, they spent one day resting the animals by a bright pond rimmed with willows.

"Carmarthen is over that hill," Ambrosius said, pointing. "But it will wait. The fair is not for two days yet. Viviane has costumes to tidy and we, my boy, we have fishing. A man—whether a mage or a murderer—can always find time to fish."

He took Hobby down to the pond and there, Ambrosius proved himself a bad angler but a merry companion. All he managed to catch was one angry turtle, but the stories he told until dark more than made up for his incompetence. It was Hobby who pulled in the one small spotted trout they roasted over the fire that night and shared three ways.

"Did you know," Ambrosius said as they banked the fire, "that the Celts in Eire believe little spotted fish can rise up out of the water prophesying? Who knows what this one might have told us."

Viviane suddenly burst in with a bubbly song:

> *"The warrrrrrrrrrters are cold,*
> *But crystal clearrrrrrrr;*
> *I rrrrrrrise to the fly*
> *And so appearrrrrrr . . ."*

"You appear to be interrupting the story," Ambrosius said, and they all laughed.

"Hobby, take these plates to the stream and rinse them. This old man needs to be taught his manners," Viviane said.

Hobby took the plates and went down to the stream. With his hands in the cold water, he began to dream. It was a dream in which he was a child again, with a mother and father rocking him to sleep, the *creak-creak-creak* of the cradle sounding suspiciously like the wheels of the green castle cart.

When he woke, his hands were like ice, and an almost full moon was reflected in silver shards in the water.

Theirs was not the only wagon on the road before dawn, but it was the gaudiest by far. Peddlers' children leaped off their own wagons to run alongside, begging the magician for a trick. He did one for each child and asked for no coins at all, even though Viviane scolded about it.

"Each child will bring another to us," he said, "once we are in the town. They will be our best criers. And those who come in Carmarthen will not get away free." He made a showy pink musk mallow appear from under the chin of a dirt-faced tinker girl, this trick even more remarkable—thought Hobby—because musk mallow was long past season. The girl giggled, took the flower, and ran off.

Viviane shook her head. It was clearly an old argument between them.

At first each trick made Hobby gasp with delight. At twelve he was still child enough to be guiled. But partway through the day he began to notice where the flowers and scarves and eggs really appeared from—out of the vast sleeves of the mage's robe. He started watching Ambrosius' hands carefully through slotted eyes and, unconsciously, began to imitate him.

Viviane reached over and slapped his fingers so hard they burned. "Here!" she said sharply. "It is bad enough he does tricks for free on the road, but you would beggar us for sure if you give his secrets away."

So, Hobby thought, there are secrets of the hand as well as the tongue. Sotto voce, indeed. He was both embarrassed and elated by Viviane's attention, and by his discovery. And, to be truthful, a bit upset that the mage's magic had less to do with some real power and more to do with imagination. Still, his quiet concentration on the mage's tricks and the constant rocking of the wagon soon combined to put him to sleep. Again he dreamed. It was a wicked, nasty dream in which Viviane was as young as he and a whitethorn tree fell upon her. When he awoke, he was suddenly afraid that the dream would come true. He wanted to warn her, but then remembered that his dreams did not seem to come true literally, but only *on the slant*. It would do no good to tell her if he did not understand the dream. That thought lent him a small amount of comfort.

If Gwethern had been a bustling little market town, Carmarthen had to be the very center of the commercial world. As they neared it, Hobby saw gardens and orchards laid out in careful squares outside the towering city walls. Some of the trees along the northern edges were ruined, the ground around them raw and wounded. There were spotty pastures where sheep and kine grazed on the fall stubble. The city walls were made up of large blocks of limestone, though who could have moved such giant stones was a mystery to him. Above the walls he glimpsed crenellated towers from which red and white banners waved gaudily in the shifting winds.

Unable to contain himself any longer, Hobby scrambled through the door of the wagon and squeezed in between Ambrosius and Viviane.

"Look!" he cried.

Viviane smiled at the childish outburst, but Ambrosius shook his head. "Not enough just to look, my boy," he said. "You must use all your senses here if we are to prosper. The eyes and ears are different listeners, but both feed into magecraft."

Viviane rolled her eyes up. "What makes an old man want to *lecture* all the time?" she said, not quite to herself.

Ambrosius ignored her. "What do you hear?"

Once Hobby had been used to listening, the year he had been alone in the woods. He had listened for danger: for the sound of dog and bear and wolf. He had listened for changes in the weather: leaves rustling, the grumble of the sky. And then for four years he had learned to listen to the sounds of the farm—to the needs of dogs and hens, horse and cows, and to make out the different cries of falcons in the mews and on the wing. But listening in a city was of a different nature altogether. "I hear noise."

Laughing, Viviane said, "*I* hear carts growling as they roll along. A tinker's cart is all a-jangle with pots. A farmer's cart groans under its load. And I hear voices, many different tongues. A bit of Norman, some Saxon, Welsh. Ah yes, and Frankish, too. There is a hawk screaming in the sky." She imitated its sound. "Ah—and a heavy clamor from behind the walls. Something being built, I would guess. And from the cursing, not going well."

Hobby listened again. He could begin to sort out the carts now, and the voices, though he did not know the tongues as Viviane did. The hawk, which he would have recognized, was either silent now or beyond his ken. But because Viviane had mentioned it especially, he could hear the heavy, rhythmic pounding. It was like a bass note grounding the entire Carmarthen song.

"Yes!" he said. "I can hear it. I can hear it all!"

"And what do you *see?*" Ambrosius asked.

Determined to match Viviane's ears with his eyes, Hobby began. His litany included wagons and wagoners, beasts straining to pull, birds in cages. He described farmers and weavers and cup makers and their wares. As they passed through the great city gate, under the portcullis, and into the street where burgess houses stood together in rows, he described them as well.

"Well done," Ambrosius said. "And what of the soldiers to your left?"

Hobby turned.

"No!" Viviane spoke the one word sharply, and Hobby turned back. "Never look directly on soldiers, highwaymen, or kings. Especially kings. It makes them nervous. You do *not* want any of them nervous. Look through the slant of your eye."

Hobby did as she instructed. "There are ten of them," he said.

"And . . ." Ambrosius prompted.

"And what?" Hobby was puzzled.

"What do they wear?"

"Why—their uniforms. And their helms. And swords. *Big* swords."

"What *color* uniforms? What *color* helms? And what *kind* of swords?" Viviane asked, exasperated.

Hating the tone of her voice, Hobby was quick

to answer. "Six are in red, with red plumes in the helms. Four in white." He took a deep breath. "I do not know what kind of swords."

"The swords are unimportant," Ambrosius said. "At least for such as we. But we need to ask ourselves why. Why are some of the soldiers sporting red plumes, and some white? Why are they in two different colors? Are there two armies here? Do they serve two different lords? And if so, why?"

"I do not know," Hobby said.

Ambrosius laughed. "I do not know either. Yet. But it is something odd to be tucked away. And I collect oddities."

Viviane laughed, too. "Thus endeth the lesson, master hawkling."

Hobby thought about the strange lessons. With Master Robin he had learned about farming, about the rounds of endless caring, a straightforward life. Mag had taught him cleanliness. And Nell—games. But Ambrosius and Viviane's lessons were more twisty somehow. And full of lies. Still, he liked being part of their company. They made him laugh.

Viviane clicked to the mules, who had slowed, and slapped their backs with the reins.

"Once around the square, fair Viviane," Ambrosius said. "Then shall we choose our place. Things are already begun. I have seen a juggler, Hugh of the Reeds, I believe. And a pair of acrobats, young but enthusiastic. And several strolling players are trying their tricks. But none, I wager, anywhere near our range. We shall do very well here, I smell it." He tapped his nose with his long right finger and smiled. "Very well indeed."

9. SECRETS

IN A SUIT OF GREENS AND GOLDS—THE GOLD a cotta of the mage's that Viviane had tailored to fit him, the green some old hose sewn over with gold patches and bells—Hobby strode through the crowd with a tambourine collecting coins after each performance.

"Our boy Hobby will pass amongst you, a small hawk among the pigeons," Ambrosius had announced before completing his final trick, the one in which Viviane was shut up in a box and subsequently disappeared, appearing again with a great flourish at the wagon's door.

Hobby had glowed when Ambrosius pronounced his name and claimed, aloud, possession of him. *Our* boy, the mage said, as if they were a family, just the three of them. As in his dream. Hobby repeated the phrase *sotto voce* and smiled. That infectious smile brought coins waterfalling into his tambourine, though he was unaware of its power.

On the third day of the fair, after their evening performance, when Viviane had sung in three different voices at the wagon's door, a broad-faced soldier with a red plume came up to them and stood carefully at attention.

He waited for the crowd to dissipate, then announced to Ambrosius: "The Lady Renwein would have you come this evening to the old palace and sends this purse by way of a promise. There will be more if the performance is satisfactory." He dropped the purse into Ambrosius' hand.

The mage bowed low and then, with a wink at Hobby, began drawing out a series of colored scarves from behind the soldier's ear. They were all shades of red: crimson, pink, vermillion, flame, scarlet, carmine, and rose.

"For your lady," he said to the soldier.

The soldier relaxed, laughed, and took them. "They are her colors. She will be pleased. Though not, I think, his lordship."

"The white soldiers are his, then?" asked Ambrosius.

The soldier grunted. It was all the answer he gave. "Be in the kitchen for dinner. You shall eat what the cook eats."

"Then let us hope," Viviane said, taking the purse from Ambrosius' hand, "that we like what the cook likes."

They packed up all they would need for the performance in two large baskets and walked toward the old palace at six of the clock, the bells ringing out the hour.

Along the wall of the old palace were ranged guards in pairs, one red and one white. Ambrosius pulled on his beard thoughtfully.

"Hobby," he asked, "when you went through the fair between our performances, did you hear any of the guards talking?"

"Not talking exactly," Hobby said. "But matching names."

"What names?"

"The red guards called the white guards things like 'Dirty Men of a Dirty Duke.'"

"And the white?"

"Must I say?" Hobby asked. "It touches on the lady's reputation."

"You must," the mage answered. "What touches her, may touch us."

"She was called Dragonlady."

"Ah," Viviane said. "And that is no good thing? I have been called worse in my time." She laughed.

Hobby felt his cheeks sting with embarrassment. "And the red guards called the Duke 'Draco.' Two dragons in the same nest might make for a difficult marriage."

"A difficult performance for us at any rate," Ambrosius said. "But hush. We near the palace gate."

10. THE PLAYERS

THE CASTLE WAS INDEED OLD. ITS KEEP, FROM the time of the Romans, stood mottled and pocked. The newer parts of the building, while colorful, were of shoddy material and worse workmanship. Ambrosius remarked on it quietly as they passed along the corridors.

"The sounds of construction we heard are not from here but for a brand-new castle," he said. "One hopes it is better built than this."

But when they reached the kitchen, the cook —with a stomach as round as a drum and a mouth that seemed always open—told them how badly that building was going. "The lady's father, the old Duke, fair beggared us fighting off imagined invaders. But then he married off his daughter to the worst invader of all, a man who fancies himself king. At least the Romans knew how to build roads and baths. We still use those that stand. But now . . ." He made the sign of horns with his right hand and spat through his fingers to ward off bad luck. "Now the countryside's in tatters from armies marching through; and the crops are hardly planted before they're thrashed down by the horses; and the new Duke making it worse building a great new house on the site of the old Roman barracks."

Viviane appeared not to listen but Ambrosius urged the cook on to more revelations. Hobby stopped attending after a while and turned his mind to the food, which was plentiful and rich. He ate so much he nearly made himself sick and curled, like a dog, three times around before settling on a cushion near the hearth. The cook's voice followed him where he lay.

"The foundation doesn't hold. What is built up by day falls down by night," the cook was saying as Hobby drifted into sleep.

A hand on his shoulder roused him, though he was still partially within his dream.

"The dragons..." he murmured, opening his eyes.

"Hush," Ambrosius said. "Hush, my boy, and remember. You called out many times in your sleep—of dragons and castles, water and blood. Remember the dream and I will tell you when to spin out the tale of it to catch the conscience of Carmarthen in its web. If I am right, there will be many coins in this." He winked and touched his finger to his nose.

Hobby closed his eyes and forced himself to remember every inch of the dream. Suddenly his hair was pulled. "Ow!" he cried, opening his eyes again.

"You are a sight!" Viviane said. "A smudge on your cheek from the hearth cushion and hair in tangles. Let me comb it." And without waiting for permission, she began running her comb through his hair.

He let her do it, of course, but it bothered him, so he tried to concentrate instead on the incredible bustle of the kitchen. The cook was now too busy to gossip with them, working at the fire: basting, stirring, turning the spit, calling out a string of instructions to his overworked crew.

"Stephen—here—more juice. Wine up to the tables and hurry, Beth, Mavis, Gwen! They are pounding their feet on the floor. That's not a good sign. The soup is hot enough—run the tureens up, and mind the handles! Use a cloth, Nan, stupid girl! And where are the sharp knives? These be dull as Saxon wit. David—step lively! The pies must come out of the oast now or they burn!"

Ambrosius stood in a corner, well away from the busyness, limbering up his fingers. Viviane began tuning her harp, concentrating with a passionate intensity that shut out everything else.

"Come, mage."

Hobby turned at the voice. It was the same soldier who had brought them to the castle, his broad, homely face now split with a smile, wine having worked its own magic.

"Come, mage. And you, singer. Her ladyship asks you to begin."

Ambrosius pointed to his baskets of apparatus. "Will you bring them up?"

Grunting, the soldier returned to his earlier gruff form, but hefted the baskets anyway. "Why not have the boy carry and fetch?"

"He can carry if he has to," Ambrosius said, "but he is much more to us than that."

The soldier laughed. "You will have no use for a tambourine boy here."

Ambrosius stood very still, letting his voice drop to a low whisper. "I have performed in higher courts than this. I know what is fit for fairs and what is fit for the Great Hall. The boy does not spill out his tricks for peasants." He moved to Hobby's side and put a hand on the boy's shoulder. "He is a reader of dreams. What he dreams comes true."

"Is that so?" the soldier asked all of them.

"It is so," Viviane said, smiling at him intimately.

Hobby closed his eyes for a moment, and when he opened them again they were the color of an ocean swell. "It *is* so."

11. DREAM-READER

VIVIANE SANG FIRST, A MEDLEY OF LOVE SONGS that favored the Duke and his lady equally. Such was her ability that each took the songs as flattering, though Hobby thought he detected a nasty undertone that made him uncomfortable. But Viviane was roundly applauded.

Deftly beginning his own performance at the moment Viviane ended hers, even cutting into her applause, Ambrosius started with silly tricks. He plucked eggs, coins, even a turtle from behind an unsuspecting soldier's ear. Hobby recognized the turtle; it was the one Ambrosius had caught when they were fishing.

Then the mage moved on to finer tricks, like guessing the name of a soldier's sweetheart, or discovering the missing red queen from a card deck under the Lady Renwein's plate. Finally he made Viviane disappear and reappear in a series of boxes, the last of which he had the soldiers thrust through with their swords. The final trick caused the soldiers much consternation, for blood appeared to leak from the boxes, though it was—Hobby knew—juices from the meat they'd had for dinner, which Viviane had kept concealed in a flask.

When she was revealed whole and hale, the hall resounded with huzzahs. The Duke smiled, whispering to Lady Renwein. She covered his hand with hers and when he withdrew his hand he held a plump purse, which he jangled at them.

"We are pleased to offer you this, mage."

"Thank you, my lord," said Ambrosius, "but we are not done yet. I would introduce you to my boy Hobby, who will tell you of a singular dream he had this day."

Hobby was led by the mage into the very center of the room. His legs trembled, but the mage whispered to him, "Do not be afraid. Simply tell the dream. Leave the rest to me."

Hobby nodded, closed his eyes as if he

dreamed still, and began. "I dreamed a tower of snow that in the day reached as high as the sky but at night melted to the ground."

"The castle!" the Duke gasped, but Lady Renwein placed her hand once more on his.

"Hush, my lord," she whispered. "This is a magician's trick. They have been in Carmarthen these three days and surely they have heard of it. It is hardly a secret."

Eyes closed, Hobby seemed not to hear them but continued on. "And then a man—a mage I think—advised them that the melted water left in the morning should be drained away. It was done as he wished, though the soldiers complained bitterly of it. At last the pool was gone and there in the mud lay two great stones, round and speckled as eggs.

"Then the mage drew a sword and struck open the eggs. In one was a dragon the color of wine, in the other a dragon the color of maggots."

There was a collective gasp from the audience, but Hobby could not stop speaking. It was as if a fever had hold of him.

"When the two dragons saw they were revealed," he said, "they turned not on the soldiers nor on the mage, but on one another. Screaming and breathing fire in the mud, they rose into the air belching smoke. At first the white had the best of it, then the red, turning over and over in the lightening sky. At last with a final clash, breast against breast, the white gashed a great hole in the red's neck and it tumbled end over end down to defeat."

At that, Hobby opened his eyes and they were the sudden green of gooseberries.

The Lady Renwein's face looked dark and disturbed. "What does that dream mean, boy?"

Ambrosius stepped between Hobby and the high table. "The boy dreams, my lady, but leaves it to me to make sense of his dreams, just as did his dear, dead mother before him."

Startled, Hobby turned to Viviane. She rolled her eyes up at the ceiling and held her mouth still.

"His mother was a dream-reader, too?" the Duke asked.

"She was," Ambrosius said, "though being a woman she dreamed of more homey things: the names of babes, the color of their eyes, and whether they be boys or girls."

Lady Renwein leaned forward. "Then say what this dream of towers and dragons means, mage."

"I will, my lady. It is of course not unknown to us that you have a house that will not stand. All the town speaks of it. However, our young Hobby has dreamed the reason for the failure. The house does not stand—in dream images it melts—because there is a pool beneath it, most likely a conduit that the Romans built for their baths. With your construction there has been leakage underground. Open the foundation of your house, drain the pool, remove or reconstruct the Roman pipes, and the building will remain whole."

"Is that all?" The Duke sounded disappointed. "I thought you might say that the red dragon was the lady's and the white mine, or some such."

"Dreams are devious, my lord," Ambrosius said, putting his hand once again on Hobby's shoulder. "Truth on the slant."

But Lady Renwein was nodding. "Yes, that makes sense, about the conduits and the drain. You need not have done all this folderol with dreams in order to give us good advice."

Ambrosius smiled, stepped away from Hobby, and bowed deeply. "But, my lady, would you have listened to a traveling magician on matters of . . . state?"

Lady Renwein smiled back, a look of perfect understanding passing between them.

"Besides," Ambrosius said, "I had not heard the boy's dream till this very moment. The cook will vouch for that. Nor have I given thought to your new home or anything else in Carmarthen, excepting the fair. It was the boy's dream that instructed us in what must be done. Like his mother, of blessed memory. She, the minx, never mentioned she was carrying a boy. Though when she had him, she said, 'He will be a hawk among princes.' And thus saying, she died. So I named him Hobby. A small hawk, but mine own."

At that Hobby started. All this talk of mothers had merely irritated him. But the fact that Ambrosius called him "mine own" made him flush with a combination of pride and embarrassment. Was there *nothing* the mage would not say for a prize?

12. A DIFFERENT READING

IT WAS TWO DAYS LATER THAT A MESSENGER arrived at the green wagon with a small casket full of coins as well as a small gold dragon pendant with a faceted red jewel for an eye.

"Her ladyship sends these with her compliments," the messenger said. "There was indeed a hidden pool beneath the foundation. And the pipes, which were grey and speckled as eggs, were rotted clear through. The Duke begs you to stay for yet another dream. He says the boy is indeed a hawk among princes."

Ambrosius smiled. "Thank them both from us and say that we will let the boy dream tonight and come tomorrow with him."

After the messenger had departed, Viviane laughed. "Hawk among princes indeed!" She ran her fingers through the coins. "Here, hawkling," she said, placing the pendant's chain over Hobby's head.

The thing lay like a cold supper on his stomach and he shivered. He had been thinking for two days about all the lies Ambrosius had told the Duke, one atop another. Yet some were lies even he wanted to believe in. A mother and father who loved him and named him. How could he be angry with the mage when that was what he most desired? Still, he had to say it, had to ask.

"You made it all up," he said. There was accusation in his voice and—to be truthful—a bit of a whine. Twelve years was not yet too old for whining. "About my mother. About the dream."

"About your mother, yes," Ambrosius admitted. "But not the dream."

"You lied."

Viviane shrugged and picked up the casket of coins. "And what of that? All magecraft is a lie," she said. "All performance. A lie, if done well, becomes truth." She placed the casket under an embroidered cloth.

"No lie in *her* performance that night," said Ambrosius. "Did you see how she managed them?" He blew her a kiss.

Viviane came over to him and touched his cheek fondly.

Hobby felt cold. They seemed quite giddy with themselves. "But you lied about the dream. It meant *nothing* like that." He wondered how he knew such a thing, but it was as if he suddenly had been given a gift of understanding simply by mentioning the dream. "Nothing."

"What do you mean?" Ambrosius asked cautiously. There was a slyness—and a fear—in his eyes that he could not disguise.

Hobby weighed his words carefully. He thought his entire future might lie in what he said next. "The dream, Ambrosius. It was not about drains."

"Ah . . ." Ambrosius let out only one small syllable.

"It was a dream about . . . armies, about the Duke's losses to come. There will be a battle, and his army will be defeated. He was right in a way. And you dismissed him."

"I did not dismiss him," Ambrosius said. "I side-stepped him. To tell a prince to his face that you have dreamed his doom invites your own. The greatest wisdom of any dreamer is to live to dream again." He smiled, but it sat on his mouth and never reached his eyes. Unaccountably his brow was spotted with sweat.

"The only duty of the dreamer is to tell the truth," Hobby said. "About the dream."

"You do not listen well," Viviane said.

"*He* does not listen at all," Hobby retorted, suddenly sure that Ambrosius had never understood the dream's meaning. The man was a charlatan through and through. The actual dream had never mattered. He would have told the Duke the same whatever the dream. Lady Renwein had the right of it. And Hobby suddenly knew something else as well: Ambrosius was afraid of both the dream and the dreamer. "You are jealous and afraid," he spat out. "You know yourself to be nothing more than a sleight-of-hander. *I* am the true dream-reader."

Ambrosius did not answer, his face drawn.

"I am sorry," Hobby said quickly. "I should not have said that." But whether he meant he was sorry for his tongue's sharpness or for saying out loud what they all already knew, none of them was sure.

Ambrosius turned and gave Viviane an unreadable look. "The boy is right about one thing. My hand is quicker than my mind. We go from here at once."

"Tomorrow is soon enough."

"Now."

"Boy," Viviane said, turning a smile on Hobby that made him flush all over. "Take these coins. Go into town. Buy yourself some token of the place. Kiss a pretty wench. Twelve years is none too soon for that." She reached into the pocket that hung from her belt and fetched out a handful of coins, much too much for an evening's entertainment. "Come back in an hour or two. No sooner. I will change this stubborn old man's mind that we all may have a good night's rest."

Hobby took the coins and went. Not to buy a token. Not to kiss a town maid. But to think long and hard about the power he had, this dreaming. And to think what it had to do with the matter of truth.

13. RESURRECTION

THE TOWN WAS QUIET, THE STALLS SHUT DOWN, the players all in their beds. The tubs and trestles on which goods had stood all day were pulled in for the night.

Hobby wandered through the empty town, sitting at last with his back to a stone watering trough, meaning to think. Instead he fell asleep and dreamed.

He dreamed three dreams. The first was of a hand pushing up through earth, as if someone long buried sought the light. A revenant, a shadow, a ghost to haunt him. He cried out and his own cry wakened him for a moment.

The second dream was not so frightening as the first. There was a bear, not much more than a cub, padding through the woods with a crown upon its head.

The third was a dream of a tree and in the dream he slept, dreaming.

A rough hand shook him awake. He swam up into the light of the torch, thinking, *It will be one of the guards. Or Ambrosius. Or Viviane,* though the touch was too rough for hers.

But when he heard the low, familiar growl of a dog, he knew that his first dream had, in its own way, come true. "Fowler," he whispered, meaning both the man and his breath. "I thought you were dead."

"You left me unconscious, boy. And we such good friends," Fowler said. "I heard about you when I arrived. Quite a performance, I was told. The Duke wants more. He's not yet satisfied."

"How did you know it was me?"

"Oh, a duke's spy has his little ways." The man laughed. "But a strange boy with eyes like gooseberries was a sign. That horse and cow a surety. You picked my pocket."

"I never . . ." Hobby's voice was more vehement than an innocent's should have been. It was because he *had* considered—if only for a moment —stealing from the foul man.

"At least you left me my boots."

"Master Robin's boots, you mean."

"Master Robin, is it? I heard his name was Ambrosius. He has as many names as you, young Hawk." Fowler smiled. In the torchlight his one good eye gleamed, the scarred eye was black as an empty socket. "I shall have to speak to your master for recompense. He took my boy, my horse, my cow. He shall have to pay me or I take it out in blood. Your blood for mine. Blood, they say, makes great bargains."

Hobby twisted in the man's hand but could not shake his hold. The dog growled.

"Up, hawkling." He yanked the boy to his feet and they marched through the shadows toward the castle on wheels.

But the green wagon was gone. Gone were the mules. And gone as well were Goodie and Churn.

Hobby wrenched free of Fowler's hand, scouring the darkness. But he did not bother to call out. He knew, from the hard stone sitting in his chest, that they had fled long since, taking his horse and cow with them. All he had of them, his new family, was the Lady Renwein's pendant and a handful of coins. Viviane had not overpaid him after all.

The chapel bell tolled midnight and Hobby willed himself not to cry.

"So they have flown the dovecote, leaving the little pigeon behind," Fowler said, his hand once more heavy on Hobby's shoulder.

Hobby did not bother to answer. Indeed, what could he have said? That he had been cozened by Viviane's smile and an evening's worth of coppers? That he had believed Ambrosius wanted him for a son? That they had run off in the end because they were afraid of him, afraid of his dreaming?

"I wonder the Duke let them go," Fowler mused aloud. "But perhaps he does not know they are gone yet. Perhaps they greased the palm of some willing gatekeeper. There may be some good to be made from this yet."

"You mean good for *you*," Hobby said.

"That is all anyone ever means, boy," Fowler said. He laughed out loud and at that his dog slapped at the ground with a paw. Neither sound was comforting. "Come, Hawk. I expect the Duke would like to know that you, at least, are safe and awake."

14. TRUE MAGIC

THEY WENT UP TO THE DUKE'S PRIVATE APART-ments by a twisting back stair. At each turning stood a stone-eyed guard, hand on sword beneath a flickering wall torch. The flames made shadows crawl up and down the stairs. Hobby could not have run, even if he dared, not because of the guards but because Fowler's hand was ever on his shoulder.

The Duke was waiting for them, sitting at a great desk near a window. He was fingering papers and his eyes were not on them. Hobby could not tell if the man was just tired or if he—like most of the nobles—was unlettered. His eyes, however, were on Hobby and his keeper, and these two he could read very well indeed.

"You have brought me the singing bird but not his handler," the Duke said. "He is no good to me without his quick-fingered interpreter, that mage."

Hobby spoke up at once. If Fowler had hoped to get something for his news, he would not. "The mage, Ambrosius, is gone. You will not find him."

"A father desert his child?" the Duke asked, then gave a short laugh, musing aloud. "The forest teems with such leavings—boys and girls without hope of family or life. Why should *your* father be different?"

Hobby looked down at the rushes on the floor. "He is *not* my father. My father was a falconer." Then he looked up, staring directly into the Duke's eyes. "Ambrosius is no real magic maker either."

The Duke leaned back in his chair and made a triangle of his fingers. "A charlatan. And you think this news surprises me?" But his face spoke differently.

Fowler chuckled.

"Are you a charlatan, too, boy?" the Duke asked.

"I do not know what I am," Hobby answered truthfully, for his magic required it.

"Are your dreams trickery then?" The Duke was like a hound on a scent.

Hobby suddenly remembered Ambrosius' warning against speaking truth to princes. Yet he knew, in his very bones, that he had to answer all direct questions of his magic directly. "My dreams come true. But on the slant."

"On the slant." The Duke closed his eyes and his voice was old. "I am not a man of such angles," he said. "We have got already what we wanted from the mage. The building stands. What more I seek, I do not rightly know. Can you tell me more, boy?"

The question was specific and Hobby knew he had no choice but to speak the truth. "There is more, sir."

"Then tell it me," the Duke said, with a sigh.

"The dragons are meant to be armies." Hobby spoke quietly but not so quietly that he could not be heard in that hush of a room. "Not your army or your wife's. But greater armies than both. There will be a battle and you will have the worst of it."

"How much worse?"

Hobby drew in a breath. He could not stop telling the dream. "You will die. Burned up in flame greater than dragon's breath."

"What battle, boy?" Fowler asked. "When?" He had drawn close to Hobby's side and breathed the questions into the boy's ear.

"My dream does not name a time or place of battle," Hobby said.

"Then, boy," the Duke said, "your dream is useless. I dream every night of battles. Some I win, some I lose. In this world there are always battles. There are always deaths. When you are a duke. When you would be a king." He stood and turned his back on the boy and the spy, staring out through the window to the blackness beyond. "I am not afraid to die cleanly, on the battlefield. But burning . . ." He shuddered. "I do not believe your slantwise dreaming. It is too tricky for an old soldier. Go away, boy. You tire me." And indeed the Duke's shoulders seemed to sag and his voice was ragged, as if torn on a nail.

"But perhaps . . ." Fowler began.

The Duke turned around abruptly, suddenly years younger in his fury. "But me no buts, Master

83

Mind-It-All. You have brought me no news from the south. No news about my enemies, about the numbers of their armies, about where they march and when. You have brought me only a charlatan, long fled, and a boy who dreams—so he says— my death by burning. *Burning!* Like a common witch. Like a warlock. *I will not hear of it."* He glared at Fowler and not at Hobby. If he had looked at the boy, his story might have ended differently. But he did not. He concentrated all his anger on the man opposite him. "I will not be fooled. I am a fighting man. I do not listen to the dreams of ragged boys. Run along, child, and find your father. If you can."

Hobby turned to leave and the dog, who had been lying at Fowler's feet, rose and walked stiff-legged toward him, the hair on the ridge of its neck rising.

"I do not believe he is an ordinary boy, my lord," Fowler said. "Neither does my dog. He is more than the son of a falconer or the boy of a wandering player. I believe we need to find out *who* he is. Test his magic. Then perhaps he will be able to tell us the time and place of battles, the time and place of . . ."

"Of my death?" The fury in the Duke's voice was controlled now, tight, and the more dangerous for it. "So you can sell that piece of information to someone else?"

"My lord, do you so mistrust me?" Fowler asked.

"You have asked too many wrong questions already and not enough right ones," the Duke said. "I would be a fool *not* to mistrust you. I am no fool."

"Just his name, my lord duke," Fowler said. But he asked it of the Duke, not Hobby.

Hobby hesitated, knowing that names held power. Though he had not been asked directly, and though it was not about a dream, it still touched on his magic. But not—he realized—directly. "I am a hawk," he said, humor hidden in his answer. "A hawk among princes."

The Duke laughed explosively as if he got the joke. "A hawk. Ah yes, I remember your name now, Hobby. Fly away, little hawk, before I change my mind."

"Hawk," said Fowler, remembering the other name, and reaching for the boy.

"Merlin," the boy whispered, but *sotto voce*,

without sound. Then, as the Duke had ordered, he flew back down the stairs and out into the night, where armies were, truly, massing on the far side of the woods.

He flew unerringly into those woods, and freedom.

Light.

Morn.

"What is that hawk, Viviane? The one circling above us. Is it a hobby?"

"There is no hawk above us, old man. There is only cloud and, beyond it, sky."

"I heard the hawk. I heard his voice."

"It was a dream."

"I never dream. Only he dreams."

"You will dream a long dream soon. About the times when your fingers were swift and sure with magic. When you could pluck asters and asphodels from a child's ear."

"I never could do magic. Not like the boy."

"Hush. There was no boy. That was only a dream. Drink this and the dream will come again. For good."

The bells in her earrings ring like the sound of a tamed hawk's jesses, like the sound of a freed soul as it makes its long and perilous passage between earth and heaven.

AUTHOR'S NOTE

The story of Merlin, King Arthur's great court wizard, is not one story but many. In some of the
tales he is a Druid priest, in others a seer, in still
others a shape-shifter, a dream-reader, a wild man
in the woods.

The only story told of Merlin's childhood
handed down from the Middle Ages is that he is
a fatherless Welsh princeling who has prophetic
dreams about red and white dragons. In the story
he tells this dream—under threat of execution—
to the usurping King Vortigern. He explains that
the dream is about Vortigern's battle tower, which
has been collapsing. Under the boy's instructions,
the tower is made to stand, but it is in that very

tower that Vortigern is then burned to death by soldiers loyal to the true king.

I have borrowed bits and pieces of that old story, reworking it to include research about traveling players and market day fairs. I have put in Viviane, who in the old tales of Merlin first seduces and then kills the old man after he has taught her all his magic, by casking him up in a tree. (Or putting him to sleep in a cave.) I have also put in Ambrosius, who, in the histories, is sometimes mentioned as the father of Arthur, sometimes as a general who began the fight to unite all Britain, sometimes as Vortigern's rival and the cause of his death. In other words, I have played around with elements of the stories as writers of "Arthuriana" have always done.

The stories and histories from that time—fifth century through the fifteenth—are like Merlin's dream, always told on the slant. The tales of Merlin are so entwined, truth and fiction, that they are tangled and impenetrable as the forests of old Britain.

—J. Y.

BENNINGTON FREE LIBRARY